Middle Row

Middle Row

Sylvia Olsen

orca soundings

ORCA BOOK PUBLISHERS

Library and Archives Canada Cataloguing in Publication

Olsen, Sylvia, 1955-
Middle row / Sylvia Olsen.
(Orca soundings)

ISBN 978-1-55143-901-3 (bound).--ISBN 978-1-55143-899-3 (pbk.)

I. Title. II Series.
PS8579.L728M53 2008   JC813'.6   C2008-900483-3

First published in the United States, 2008
Library of Congress Control Number: 2008921116

Summary: In the face of ignorance and racism, Vince and Raedawn try
to find out what has happened to a missing classmate.

*Orca Book Publishers is dedicated to preserving the environment and has printed
this book on paper certified by the Forest Stewardship Council®.*

Orca Book Publishers gratefully acknowledges the support for its publishing
programs provided by the following agencies: the Government of Canada
through the Canada Book Fund and the Canada Council for the Arts,
and the Province of British Columbia through the BC Arts Council
and the Book Publishing Tax Credit.

Cover photography by Getty Images

ORCA BOOK PUBLISHERS
PO Box 5626, Stn. B
Victoria, BC Canada
V8R 6S4

ORCA BOOK PUBLISHERS
PO Box 468
Custer, WA USA
98240-0468

www.orcabook.com
Printed and bound in Canada.

14 13 12 11 • 6 5 4 3

For my children, who have taught me so much about the middle row.

Before I Start

The seating on the bus is different this year. That's because Raedawn and I and Sherry and Steve crossed the line. As white as I am, I sit up front with Raedawn and the First Nations kids. And as First Nations as Steve is, he sits at the back with Sherry and the other white kids. That's just the way it is now that we're going out. People on both sides might not like it, but that's too bad.

Nick and Justin took a little time to adjust to the new situation. I've left them in the back row with Steve and Sherry. They're choked I don't spend all my time with them. They don't get it—when you get a girlfriend, things change. Oh, and the other thing: Steve thinks he owns the back seat. Nick and Justin might be able to tolerate him sitting there if he didn't sprawl halfway across as if he's now the king of the bus.

Things have changed on the bus. The trouble is that the middle row, always reserved for Dune, has been empty since the first day of school—ten days ago.

Chapter One

The bus pulls over for the kids from the reserve in front of Ruby's convenience store. Raedawn jumps on in front of the others. She hurries down the aisle and drops into the seat beside me. She's excited and out of breath as if she's in a hurry to sit on the bus for the boring forty-five-minute ride to school. She drags her backpack up onto her lap.

"Wait till you see what Mom bought me on the weekend," she says, unzipping the bag. "You won't believe it."

She tugs on something from inside until a new soccer boot springs free.

"Look at this baby."

She holds the boot in front of my face until I laugh.

"What's so funny?"

"That can't possibly fit your foot," I say. "My feet haven't been that small since I was in grade one."

She takes a swing at me.

She says, "Doesn't mean I'm not fast." Her eyes light up. "I got the treads. I got the gear. And I'm going to be the starting center this year. I am. I am. I am."

"I believe you. I believe you. I believe you," I say, mimicking her.

"We're going to be the city champs." She punches the air.

I put my ankle on my knee. She does the same. We press the soles of our feet together. Her foot is almost exactly half as long as mine. But then, they don't call me Mr. Hoops for nothing. The last shoes I bought were size thirteen.

"You got monster feet." She laughs. "They're too big to play soccer. You'd trip over them."

"Oh yeah? When was the last time you saw me trip over my feet playing basketball?"

She thinks. "Okay. Never, I guess. But no one in the whole world could possibly need a pair of feet that big."

She starts talking about random stuff. Twenty minutes later we get to the hairpin turn. Raedawn stops talking in mid-sentence. The bus rumbles around the corner and over the bridge. It hums along the straight stretch, tires swishing on the wet pavement past the place where Dune usually waits. On a normal day the bus would have pulled over on the gravel shoulder and groaned to a stop. Dune would have hopped on. He would have walked down the aisle, nodding at some of the kids at the front of the bus without looking straight at anyone. He'd have gone to the middle row—the same place he's sat since as far back as I can remember. The seat everyone leaves empty for him.

Not this morning.

Raedawn stays quiet until Dune's stop is out of sight.

"Vince," she says. She twists around and looks out the back window as if she's going to see him running behind. "Dune hasn't been at school since the first day. This is the tenth day. Don't you think that's strange?"

"Not really. His mom probably got sick of living in the bush and moved away."

"He's lived out here as long as you have lived in town. Wouldn't it be kind of weird if your family just got tired of it and moved away?"

"I guess so."

"Yeah, well my family wouldn't just up and move off the reserve either. People around here don't do that."

I say, "But Dune's family is kind of messed up anyway," which is a huge understatement.

I don't know anything about his family really. Only that they live halfway between our town and the town where we go to school. It is a forty-five-minute drive from the edge of the Pacific Ocean to the west through clear-cuts and forest to the east. Past the school it takes another forty-five minutes to get to the city. So what I'm saying is that Dune lives in the middle of nowhere. And as far as I know, the only family Dune has is his mother.

She's another story—she looks like a hippie. She has long stringy blond hair and wears big skirts and work boots. Everyone says they live in a shack that she built herself. No one knows exactly where it is. It's either down the hill by the beach or up the mountain somewhere in the forest. The only thing we know for sure is that they must live near the bridge where he waits for the school bus. Another thing about the place is that there's no electricity, telephone, cable, no cell phone reception or even a driveway that you can see from the road.

Dune's got no friends at school that I know of. At lunch he's either in the art room or hanging out on a bench in the hall doodling. He doesn't talk to anyone. I've bumped into him and his mom at the grocery store in town a few times. They throw me an odd kind of smile and then look away like they're worried I'm going to want to talk to them. No worries. I seriously doubt that's going to happen anytime soon.

Raedawn says, "Something's wrong." She's talking quietly. "It doesn't feel right."

"What's there to be wrong? A guy doesn't come to school. It wouldn't be the first time."

She says, "Okay, but what if something is wrong? Who's going to know?"

"His family, his friends. There's gotta be people," I say, wishing she'd just drop the subject.

"You ever seen him with friends?"

"No."

"Me neither."

She gets quiet again until the bus stops at the school.

She says, "Something's wrong. And I'm going to find out."

Chapter Two

It turns out that Raedawn went to the office and made up some lame story about needing to get in touch with Dune. She asked the secretary if Dune had quit school. No, he hadn't. And did the secretary have a contact number for him? No, she didn't. Then how did the school contact him? The secretary pulled up his files on her computer screen and checked everything they had on him. They had never contacted his home. Not as far as anyone in the office could remember.

It's not good enough for Raedawn. After school she drags me down to Mr. Blaney's office. He's the school counselor.

"Come on," she says. "If anyone's gonna know about Dune, it'll be him."

The last thing I want to do is go to a shrink—for any reason. And anyway, what's all this got to do with me? Dune's business is not my business.

She says, "Sit here." She plops down on a chair near the door.

I'm pacing up and down the hall, thinking of ways to get out of what's coming up. It's not Dune I'm worried about. I don't want to get caught with Raedawn outside Mr. Blaney's office. I can already hear the gossip. *First he gets a girlfriend from the reserve and*

*then they're off to relationship coun-
seling.* I can hear the guys splitting their
guts laughing.

"Where are you going?" she asks.

"Nowhere." I'm edgy. Looking around
the halls. "But this isn't my game. Why
don't we just leave this thing alone?"

Raedawn's fidgety. I can tell she isn't
thinking of what people are going to
say about us or of whose business it is.
She's starting to freak out that Dune is
really in trouble.

She says, "Someone's gotta know
something about him."

"You're right. So let them find him."

"Vince! Don't you even care?"

"I don't know anything about him.
He's not a friend of mine."

"That's not the point. Maybe he
doesn't have any friends. Maybe someone
needs to be his friend. Maybe he's in
trouble and needs help. Don't you ever
think about stuff like that?"

I say, "Okay, okay. I'm here, aren't I?"

I learned a few things about Raedawn from going out with her all summer. Once something gets stuck in her head, she won't let it go. And if someone's in trouble, she has to help. Like the day we went in the ambulance to the hospital with a kid who busted his arm. Raedawn couldn't find his mother, so guess who took over? Raedawn. And guess who ended up wiping the kid's snotty face with a cold cloth? Me. At least no one caught me playing nurse.

"Can I help you two?" Mr. Blaney asks when he's coming down the hall.

"I just have a few questions," Raedawn says.

"Great, come on in." He opens the door and shoots me one of those sappy can-I-help-you-son looks. It creeps me out and I want to get out of there. Then I step up to him, shake his hand and the weirdest words fall out of my mouth.

"We're worried about Dune." I can't believe I said that.

Raedawn's jaw is hanging open. She can't believe I said it either.

"Yeah," she says, pulling herself together. "He hasn't been at school since the first day. That was almost two weeks ago."

Mr. Blaney strokes his chin. He glances from Raedawn to me and back. I can tell he's in a bind. Confidentiality. Teachers aren't allowed to tell personal junk about one student to another. The guy can't decide what to do. Not that I care about him. I'm just glad the door's shut and I'm out of sight.

He flicks the end of his nose with his finger a few times and says, "No, he hasn't. I noticed that as well."

Raedawn says, "He hasn't withdrawn."

"No? Do you know that for sure?"

Raedawn looks him straight in the eye.

"Do you know what might be wrong with him?" she asks.

He says, "No."

"Have you looked into it?"

"No, but I will."

She says, "How will you look into it? He doesn't have any contact numbers."

Concern floats across the shrink's face.

"Can you think of anyone who might know where Dune is?" Raedawn asks.

"I'll see what I can do. But it won't be easy. Dune and his mother stick to themselves you know."

"I know that," she says. "But I want to find him."

If Raedawn ever wants to know what she should be when she grows up, I say she should try being an investigative reporter. She's got what it takes. No stone left unturned.

Mr. Blaney says, "Oh, I don't think you need to find him, Raedawn. I'll take care of this."

"Yeah, right, he'll take care of this," she says as we walk out. "He knew more than he told us."

"I thought so too." I check the hall to make sure it's clear.

"I don't think he's going to do a thing about it, Vince. You and I have to find Dune."

"Great. Just how are we gonna do that?"

"This weekend we'll go for a hike down by the bridge. If we can find his place, we should be able to find him and his mother. Maybe he's sick or something."

"Maybe he quit school."

"I doubt it. He gets straight A's. He's going to get scholarships this year."

"Good luck on that one. He looks more like a dropout. "

"Maybe if you took the time to talk to him, you'd know that he plans on moving out of here as soon as he gradu-ates. He's going to go to university and study climate change. He's a total science freak."

"How do you know so much?"

"I talk to him whenever I get a chance. He doesn't say much, but I get some stuff out of him."

Raedawn's probably the only person alive who knows anything about Dune. That's the weird thing about her; she's actually interested in people.

Me, on the other hand, I know that Dune is one strange guy. He draws bugs and insects and junk like that. And that's as much information as I need.

Chapter Three

On Saturday Raedawn hooks us up a ride with one of her uncles. He pulls up to my house in a Jeep with a kid in the front seat. I jump in the back with Raedawn.

"This is Isaiah, my nephew," she says all cheerfully even though it's not even 9:00 AM. "And you've met Uncle Curtis before, right?"

I nod. I can't remember when, but she must be right. Either way I'd just as soon skip the introductions.

"Jump in, Stretch," Uncle Curtis says. Since meeting the people on Raedawn's reserve, I've become Stretch. Other than her Uncle Dave, who I only saw once at a distance, the guys in her family are seriously short—up to my pits, if they're lucky.

He asks, "Soooo, what did you kids say you were doing today?"

"We're going to find Dune," Raedawn says. "He's a guy from school. He lives out by the bridge somewhere but he's missing. He hasn't been at school since the first day."

"I think I know who you mean. His mother used to hang around town years ago. She built a squatter's hut down by the beach. I think the government shut her down a couple of years ago. But she's moved back in somewhere. I still

19

see her every once in a while. She sells art to the gallery."

"You know anything about her kid?" Raedawn asks.

He says, "Not really." He gives us a glance that reminds me of how Mr. Blaney looked—he knows something he's not telling us. "Other than he's a scruffy-looking kid."

Raedawn wants to find out *where* Dune is. But what's really burning her up is *who* he is. Or rather, who his father is. Everyone wants to know the answer to that question. There are a million stories.

My dad's story goes something like this: Dune's mom breezed into town about eighteen years ago looking like something right out of a magazine. Blond hair, blue eyes, long legs. The old man practically drools when he mentions her legs. As far as Dad is concerned, all she had to do was look at a guy and he was sure she wanted him. After Dad and his friends have had a few drinks, they get pretty disgusting when they talk about her.

Raedawn asks, "Is her name really Ocean?"

"That's the only name I've heard," Uncle Curtis says. "But then, she was a hippie chick, so maybe her name's really Geraldine." He laughs.

I say, "Good luck finding her, if we don't even know her real name."

"Good luck," Uncle Curtis says, stopping the car on the gravel at the side of the bridge. "You got something to keep you dry? It's going to rain."

I jump out.

"We're fine," Raedawn says. She scoots across the backseat and out the door. "Just don't forget to pick us up at three o'clock."

He looks at me, lifts his chin toward Raedawn and says, "That's some girl you got there, Stretch. Hope you can keep up to her."

"Yeah, thanks," I say, beginning to understand what he means. It's dense bush on both sides of the road. The last thing I want to do is chase Raedawn around the woods looking for someone I don't even care about. This is her freakish idea. If I had my way, I'd be lying in bed.

"Bye, Raedawn," the kid yells.

She calls back, "Bye, honey face."

Uncle Curtis gives me a thumbs-up and drives away.

"Let's head down to the beach first," Raedawn says. "With names like Ocean and Dune, I figure they moved back down there after the government evicted them."

"You could be right," I say. The beach is a long way from the road, but it looks like it will be an easier hike than heading up into the forest.

We look around for a while and find a trail that's overgrown and covered with fallen trees.

Raedawn says, "This has got to be the old trail." She climbs over a monster fallen cedar. "I think there's a newer trail to the beach around here somewhere, but I think it would be pretty cool to find out where the beach people used to live."

I say, "Dad calls them worse than that."

"Yeah, well, so much for your dad," she says. "He calls me worse than that as well."

You have to be careful what you say and do when Raedawn's around—'cause when she gets messed up, you're in trouble. That's where Dad's got a problem. Screwing around with people's heads is his favorite sport. He gets some kind of sick pleasure out it. Raedawn never lets me forget that my old man's an idiot. It's her job, she says, to make sure I don't turn out like him.

"It's been a while since anyone has used this trail," she says, kicking ferns out of her way.

I say, "Isn't it sort of obvious that they don't live down here anymore?"

"Maybe, but at least if we follow this trail we'll know where they used to live. We'll know what sort of place we are looking for."

It's a useless plan, but I keep my mouth closed.

Raedawn starts running the obstacle course—no trouble—jumping windfalls and mud holes. Not me. It's too much like hunting with Dad when I was a kid. *Hurry the hell up. What the hell are you waiting for? Do you think we have the whole damn day?*

I stumble around after her, getting farther and farther behind.

She calls, "Look," and disappears into the woods. "Vince! Look!"

I follow the sound of her voice to a clearing with a broken-down shack. In front, weathered log benches circle around what looks like a barbecue pit made out of a pile of beach stones.

The place is not normal, but I'm happy enough to sit on one of the benches. As soon as I do, my head gets full of images of bearded guys and long-haired women sitting cross-legged, singing and playing guitars.

"Vince." Raedawn's voice comes from inside the shack. "Come on in here. You aren't going to believe it."

I hunch over to get in the door. Old lace curtains droop at the windows. There's a rusted woodstove in the corner of the room. The chimney, half disinte-grated, has fallen through the hole in the roof. There's a sink with no faucets and beach-stone mosaics everywhere, on the walls, counters, floor. A couple of wooden bed frames without mattresses lean against the walls.

Raedawn says, "This is where they lived."

"How do you know? They weren't the only beach bastards who lived down here."

"Vince!" she snarls. "What did you call them?"

"Sorry."

"See, there you go sounding like your father again."

That's the trouble with living with a bigoted fathead like my dad. The same junk he says just spews out of my mouth before I have time to think. I didn't have a clue how bad he was until I started hanging out with Raedawn. Now I realize half the stuff I say is just as gross as him.

She turns away and I follow her outside. We sit on the bench.

There's some kind of crazy romance hanging around in the air. I start thinking about moving away from home and building a shack like this one for Raedawn and me. A secret little place where we could be alone.

"Imagine." She's looking at the barbecue and snuggling up beside me. I like it. She grabs my hand. "Imagine living here."

Damn, this is good, I'm thinking. She's feeling the same stuff as me.

I say, "Yeah. I know what you mean."

"I figure Dune lived here until he was about twelve years old, and then they got evicted."

She drops my hand and sits up. She makes it pretty clear that she's not thinking about romance.

"No water, no electricity, no TV, no computer." She sighs. "No traffic, no neighbors, no family, no telephone."

"That's messed up." I figure that list pretty much eliminates everything that's any fun. "What did he do with his time?"

It starts to rain, so we push back on the bench under the trees to keep dry. Raedawn reaches behind the bench and picks up a hunk of cedar about the size of my leg. It's carved like a totem pole, but the images look like cartoon characters—a dog on the bottom with bugs and insects sitting one on top of the other.

She says, "Wow. This is what Dune did with his time. Vince, this is beautiful. It's just like the stuff he draws."

She strokes the pole like she's petting a kitten and gets a glazed-over look on her face.

"Here." She passes the thing to me.

I grab it. This is totally weird. As soon as I touch it I start looking around, checking over my shoulders. For all I know there could be people hanging around a place like this. Dune and his mother might be hiding out in the bushes. Or some of the other beach bastards. Who knows what they're up to. I toss the thing back to Raedawn.

"Let's get the hell out of here."

Along the beach we find other trails leading to deserted shacks but none as big as the first one. When we meet up with Curtis back by the bridge, we're soaking wet and starving.

He asks, "Find anything?"

"Yeah," Raedawn says. "Old shacks. Nothing new."

"What do you have there?"

"Dune's totem pole." She holds it up so they can see it in the front.

Curtis says, "Let me look at that thing." Raedawn pushes it over the seat. He does the same thing as her. He runs his fingers over the pole like it's magic or something. "What a thing! How do you know it's his?"

"He draws stuff like that in class. The very same animals."

The kid says, "That's a cool-looking dog."

He's right. There's no doubt the guy is a good artist. But the whole thing is creepy as far as I am concerned.

Chapter Four

"Where the hell you been?" Dad's sitting on the front steps having a smoke.

"The beach."

He takes a puff. "What beach?" He waits a few seconds and blows the smoke my way. "And who the hell was driving that Jeep?"

"The beach by the bridge," I say and pass him at the front door. "And that was Raedawn's Uncle Curtis."

"What the hell you doing with that bunch?"

"Raedawn is my girlfriend, remember?"

"We raised you right, Vincent, your mother and I. I thought you'd do better than this. But hell, look at you."

"Look at me what?"

He follows me into the kitchen.

Things are black and white with the old man—his way or no way. We fought like hell about Raedawn for a few months until I gave up. There was no point. Apparently I was a disgrace to the family. Which is a joke when you think about it. Like our family ever had any grace.

Dad decided I can live in the house until I graduate, and then I gotta take off like Ronny, my older brother, did.

Fine with me. I can't wait. And Raedawn isn't allowed over. Also fine with me. It's not like Raedawn wants to come to our insane house anyway. Mom pretends she doesn't agree with Dad, but she's as bad as he is. She's just been to town a few more times and knows it's not so cool to say so.

"What the hell were you doing at the beach?"

"Nothing."

He says, "Hell nothing. No one goes down there for nothing."

"What do you know about it?"

He's standing so close I can smell the smoke on his breath. I slap a few peanut butter sandwiches together.

"That's where that old hippie chick and the rest of those lazy beach bastards lived until a few years ago when the government finally got the balls to throw them out."

"That old hippie chick must be about your age."

"What's your point, smart-ass? If she's my age you'd think she'd have grown up a little. Got a job. Like an adult."

"Looks like she does just fine to me."

"That's just my point. They don't do anything at all. They take what they can get and live off the rest of us. No work, no taxes. Why do you think the government gave them the boot?"

"She's an artist," I say. I wonder why I'm sticking up for her. "You can see her stuff at the gallery."

In the living room, I switch on the golf channel and eat the sandwiches. The last thing I want to do is talk to the old man. Dune and his mother are getting to me. The sight of the shack and the pole and the barbecue pit are stuck in my head.

He says, "Give me that remote." He flops into his recliner and kicks his feet up. "I'm not watching that stupid game."

"Then don't. But I am."

Any other day, Dad would have gone ballistic. Instead he cracks a beer and stares at Tiger Woods.

"What'd you go down there for?"

"Looking for Dune." I decide to find out what he knows.

"What the hell kind of name is Dune?"

"He's the hippie chick's son."

Dad laughs. He says, "I guess a woman with a name like Ocean would call her damn son Dune."

He cracks another beer. "Why are you hanging out with him now? First it's Indians and now it's beach bastards."

"Shut up with those names. Why don't you lay off the crap talk about people?" I say. "And I'm not hanging with him. I'm looking for him."

"Why are you looking for him? Is he lost?"

"I don't know. He hasn't been to school since the first day and usually he never misses."

"Last time I saw his mother, she was with a greasy biker with one of those dumb-ass kerchiefs on his head. Looked like a gangster. From what I remember, Ocean was all about peace and love. What a bunch of bull."

"When was that?"

"A few weeks ago. Maybe. At the gas station in town."

"Have you ever seen the guy before?"

"Can't say that I have."

He's gulping beer as fast as he's talking.

"It's a crying shame really." He stops drinking. "She was one beautiful girl. Wasn't a man around who didn't want her."

"Who got her?"

"Don't know for sure. She hung around down at the point. There were other hippies hanging around at the same time, but she's the one you'd remember. Then she disappeared. Next time we saw her she was packing that kid around, and we heard they'd built shanties down the coast a ways."

"Whose kid?"

"Now that, sonny boy, is the million-dollar question. Everyone looked long and hard at that kid to figure it out. Your mother thought he looked like Danny Milligan down the street. But of course he won't own up to a thing. And I got my doubts that she'd have let him anywhere near her. Some people said the kid showed a bit of a likeness to Ruby's dead husband, but who's going to mention that now? I thought he looked like one of those guys down on the reserve. I don't know which one.

They all look the same. But that kid was browner than a berry when he was little."

"Did Ocean ever get married?"

"Not as far as I know. She's on her own every time I see her. Except for that biker creep the other week."

I get up to make another sandwich and wonder what just happened. Dad and I talking like two mature adults is not something I'm used to.

Dad is quiet for a few minutes. Then he says, "Hell, don't you be looking for that kid. Do you hear me?"

I can tell from the tone of his voice that our grown-up conversation is over. I grab a carton of milk and head downstairs to my room.

"Yeah, I hear you."

Chapter Five

I wake up. I hear voices upstairs. It's Raedawn.

Half asleep, I roll off the bed and open the door.

She says, "I just want to see Vince for a few minutes."

"Little girl, you are not welcome here. Didn't Vince tell you that?" Dad's bellowing like a drunk.

I drag myself up the stairs. He's at the front door. She's on the porch.

"Mr. Hardy, I'm not asking to be welcome. I'm asking to see Vince. If you want, I'll wait on the street. Just tell him I'm here."

"What's going on?" I ask.

Dad's got himself braced in the doorway like he's ready for Raedawn to make a run at him.

I give him a push. He shoves me back into the house.

"I told you that this girl isn't to be coming around here," he says. He throws his elbow against my chest, pinning me to the wall.

I say, "This girl's name is Raedawn. Now get out of my way."

"Vince." She's standing on her tiptoes, looking around Dad as if the worst he's doing is blocking her view. "Mom says she thinks she might know where Dune and his mom live. She heard

40

they live up the hill, not down by the beach. There's a logging road about five minutes from the bridge toward town."

I spring past Dad.

"Has your mom been up there?" I ask.

He snatches my arm.

"Get her out of here." Dad's face is blotchy. He's cracked a few more beer while I was asleep. "I told you not to look for that kid."

Raedawn pays no attention to Dad and carries on talking. "Mom says we should talk to Uncle Dave. He went out with Dune's mom. Can you believe that?"

Dad's going nuts.

"Listen to me, little girl. I know your Uncle Dave. He is nothing but a drunken pothead. Don't you come around here talking crap. No one in this house gives a rat's ass about your Uncle Dave or those beach bastards."

41

He lunges onto the porch toward Raedawn. She ducks. Dad grabs the rail and stops himself taking a header down the stairs.

He recovers enough to say, "You better go home where you belong."

"Or what, Dad? Or what will you do?" I push him toward the door. "Go inside and mind your own business." I go down the stairs with Raedawn. "Why don't you just shut up and stop embarrassing yourself?" I say over my shoulder.

"Vince, you gotta come with us tomorrow." She has only one thing on her mind—finding Dune. It's as if Dad is nothing more than a fly buzzing around her head.

I say, "I'm sorry about Dad."

He's worse than a distraction to me. I can't believe that I'm related to him. I shouldn't be surprised. He's acted the same way all my life. The difference now is that I know Raedawn. I mean, I really know her. It's me that's changed. I don't see things like I used to. Especially Dad. I used to think he was normal. Now everything he does drives me crazy.

She says, "I'm sorry about your dad as well, Vince. Just promise me that you won't turn out like him and I'll be okay."

I hug her. Dad shows up back on the porch with his shoes on.

"I'm warning you, Vince." He's slobbering.

I pull her toward me and hug her again right in front of him. I have to. It sounds corny but she's so good compared to him. I want to show him whose side I'm on.

"I won't, Raedawn. I promise. I won't ever turn out like him." I'm pretty sure there's no chance of me ending up like the old man. Not now.

He shouts, "You two better get the hell out of here."

While he's looking right at us, I kiss her hard and long on the lips. He can't take any more, so he staggers back into the house, slams the door. I hear the deadbolt turn.

Raedawn says, "Now what? You don't even have a jacket on. You're gonna get soaked."

"The basement door is open."

She says, "Let's go. I phoned Uncle Dave and told him I'm coming over."

She follows me to my room. I grab my coat and we walk in the rain to the reserve.

Raedawn and I usually meet in neutral places like the beach or by the river. When I go to the reserve, I am sort of invisible. Even though you can't miss me because I'm so much taller than anyone, no one says a word to me. They aren't flat-out rude like Dad, but they aren't exactly friendly either. They talk *about* me—Stretch this or Stretch that. Not *to* me. I stay pretty much out of their way. Raedawn's mom is cool, but I can tell that she doesn't think it's good that Raedawn is dating a white guy.

Chapter Six

The reserve is nothing more than a couple of streets with a few houses, a community hall and an office building. There is a field with a broken-down backstop near the beach, and a campground that no one uses anymore. That's about it. No one goes down there unless they live there, and if you're white, it's by invitation only.

By the time we get there it's almost dark. Kids are scooting around the potholes on bikes and skateboards.

"Hey, Jordan," Raedawn says to a little girl wobbling along on roller-blades. "That looks pretty hard to do."

Another kid calls, "Hey, Raedawn."

"Michael, how's your mom?"

"Not so good."

"Tell her I say hi."

Raedawn knows every kid on the street, and it's easy to see they think she's pretty cool.

Uncle Dave lives at the far end of the reserve in a rusty aluminum trailer.

I ask, "Is he going to be okay with me coming around?"

"Don't worry about Uncle Dave," she says. "He's different than anyone else on the reserve. Actually, he's different than anyone else in the whole world." She laughs.

I'm not sure I want to know what she means.

"Maybe he's not home. There's no car."

"He doesn't have a car. He walks everywhere. He thumbs to town and brings back stacks of books from the library. All he does is read and listen to music. This guy knows everything about everything."

She raps on the door. There's a light on, but it doesn't feel like anyone's home. We wait. She raps again. After a while the door opens a bit at a time. A man as tall as me grins and grabs my hand.

"Welcome to my digs."

He throws his arms around Raedawn, lifting her up like she's a little kid and swinging her around.

He says, "It was good to get your call. You haven't been over for moons. And you brought this fine young man."

We kick off our wet shoes and hang our coats on hooks by the kitchen table.

"Come on. I've got some vittles ready for you."

We follow him down two stairs into an addition at the back of the trailer.

"You need a sweater or something? You cold?" He's looking at me.

I say, "I'm fine."

Raedawn throws a blanket over her shoulders.

The room isn't much wider than a hallway. Both sides have low shelves packed with books on the top and LP records, hundreds of them, on the bottom. In the middle of the wall, between posters of guys like Gandhi and Nelson Mandela, there are words written with thick black felt pen on the bare paint:

Only two things are infinite, the universe and human stupidity, and I am not sure about the former. —Albert Einstein.

There's a woodstove and candles burning. He turns on some seventies music.

He says, "I hear Raedawn has found herself a basketball star." He points to the sofa. "You don't want to be standing there all night. Sit your bottom down and make yourself comfortable."

The coffee table is covered with plates of food—avocados, salmon, crackers, cheese, nuts, raisins.

"I got those avocados a few days ago. Never eat them. Must have been thinking of you."

I hope he isn't expecting me to eat, especially the avocados.

"I love your place, Uncle," Raedawn says. She takes a long deep breath and picks up a piece of fish with her fingers. The place smells like incense. "I gotta come around more often. Remember when you used to get me books from the library and I'd come over every Saturday to pick up new ones?"

He says, "I'd never forget that. I've got a stack of them for you to read. In fact, I've got one right here you can take with you today. It's about colonial bugs." He laughs. "They are aggressive insects, just like those Europeans. They move into regions, cause havoc for the indigenous species, take over and then off they go looking for the next place to conquer. It sounds boring, but if you can get through it, it's interesting stuff."

"Thanks." Raedawn leafs through the book as if she's really going to read it.

Uncle Dave says, "Now tell me, girl. How's soccer? I bet you're a star."

The peanut butter sandwiches have worn off, so I edge in on the food while they talk about soccer. Crackers and cheese.

Uncle Dave leans back in his recliner. "Now what can I do for you two?"

Sylvia Olsen

"We're looking for Dune. Mom says you're the one to talk to," Raedawn says. "She says you knew Dune's mom years ago."

"Okay, okay. Start from the beginning, my girl. Who is this Dune and where does he come from?" Uncle Dave looks a bit like Mr. Blaney and Uncle Curtis—he knows more than he's saying.

"Dune's mother is Ocean. Mom says you used to be tight with her."

Uncle Dave leans forward and squints. He looks as if he's thinking one thing and going to say another.

He says, "Ocean? Okay, now I did used to know that woman. And yes, I have seen her in town with a boy from time to time. But she doesn't talk to me. In fact, she makes a serious point of not talking to me. It's one of those regrets I have about my past that won't go away."

He doesn't say any more. He stares out the window. I'm thinking maybe he's already at the end of the story. He grabs a handful of nuts, tosses them in his mouth and chews slowly as if he has nothing else to do. He wipes his mouth with the back of his hand.

"We partied hard in those days. We were a bunch of wild Indians. One day Ocean breezes into the village—her and a few others like her—and sets up a tent at the campsite. She was a hippie chick straight out of the sixties, but it was 1991. It was love at first sight. She was as beautiful as a wild flower. She played the guitar and sang old protest songs. She was as good as Buffy Sainte-Marie. I romped around after her like a young buck until one night my dreams came true. We spent some time together for a few weeks. Those were the best few weeks of my life. Then as quick as she arrived, she disappeared. The next thing

I know, she's living down on the beach by the bridge with a bunch of hippies. Now whenever I bump into her she turns the other way—like I got something real bad that she could catch."

"So you were really in love with her," Raedawn says intently.

He brightens up and laughs.

"Oh, I wasn't that special. Me and every other man on both sides of the ditch—Native and white—were in love with her. Probably every man that's ever met her has fallen in love with her. But I was one loud obnoxious Indian who drank too much. Oh, and I was married at the time and she found out."

Raedawn gasps. "Uncle, I didn't know you were ever married. That's awful! How could you?"

"Yeah, sunshine. I'm not real proud of those days. I was married once and to a fine woman. But I didn't take to marriage well. I'm a late bloomer, honey. I've finally straightened up."

"Do you think Ocean loved you?"

"I don't know." He gets up. "I'm going to make some mint tea. Anyone want some?"

Raedawn says, "Sure. What about you, Vince?"

"Sure," I say.

Why not drink mint tea? By now I'm eating avocados and smoked salmon with nuts and raisins. It's the weirdest place I've ever been, and Uncle Dave's like he's from some other planet. So I might as well try mint tea. I can't imagine anyone's going to find out.

He calls from the kitchen, "I played basketball when I was in high school. I was pretty good too. Stood head and shoulders taller than any of the other guys around here. Let me know when you have a game. I'd love to watch."

I say, "Yeah, sure. I'll do that."

"Enough of my stories. What about this kid Dune?" he says, coming in with a tray of cups and a teapot.

Raedawn explains, "He's missing. We've gone to school together since kindergarten. The bus picks him up just past the hairpin by the bridge. He never misses. But this year he only came the first day, and we haven't seen him since. That's almost two weeks."

"Maybe they've finally moved out of the bush."

"No, I don't think so. Why would he come for a day and then not again?"

Uncle Dave says, "Why don't you ask his friends?"

"He's a loner. He talks to me in class, sometimes, only if I talk first. I never see him talking to anyone else. He reads books and draws."

"Why don't you ask the school? Maybe he has withdrawn and you just don't know about it."

"I did." Raedawn sounds frustrated. She thought her uncle was going to be more help. "I asked at the office. The secretary said she couldn't tell me anything about him. I told her I had an assignment of his from last year and I had to get it to him. She said as long as it had something to do with school she'd give me his address. So she pulled his records up on the screen and said 'Dune Solomon Hunter, General Delivery.' Big help she was."

Uncle Dave bounces up in his chair like he has springs in his hips.

"What did you say his name was?"

"Dune Solomon Hunter. Pretty odd name, don't you think?"

"And how old is this boy?"

"Same age as me I guess. He's in grade twelve."

"What does that make him? Seventeen?"

"Somewhere around there."

Uncle Dave chills back. But now he's all ears.

"What do you mean, missing?"

"We don't know, and we can't find out anything about him."

"Well, we better check it out."

"Really, Uncle, you'll help us find him?"

"I trust your instincts. You know I do. If you think he's in trouble, we better look for him. I'll do it for old-times sake."

After Raedawn describes the details of our useless search earlier in the day, the two of them decide that, on Sunday, Uncle Dave will borrow Raedawn's mother's car. This time we'll go up the hills into the clear-cuts and forest. Uncle Dave seems to know something about the people living up there.

Chapter Seven

On Sunday I grab a hunk of bread and a couple of oranges and gulp down half a carton of milk. I get back downstairs without having to suffer an encounter with my parents. When I get outside, Uncle Dave and Raedawn are waiting in front of the house in an old Dodge.

He says, "Morning, Vince."

Raedawn pushes over and we sit three in the front. "We're going to find him today. I just know it. But I'm scared," she says.

Uncle Dave asks, "Why are you scared?"

"Something's wrong, Uncle. I know it is."

"He'll be fine," Uncle Dave says.

"Once we find him," says Raedawn.

A few minutes past the bridge, Uncle Dave pulls up a logging road that you can hardly see from the main road. We drive through a narrow stand of trees into a recent clear-cut and head up the hill. After ten minutes dodging potholes, I realize we're definitely not in the right car. The back end keeps hitting the ground and I'm imagining walking home.

Uncle Dave's thinking the same thing.

He says, "We better park this thing and walk. If we bottom out one too many times, we'll be leaving this old baby up here and hiking back."

He throws the gearshift into park and scans the mountainside above us.

He says, "Looks like they replanted this cut about five years ago." He points to one side of the road. The hillside is covered with what look like Christmas trees. "This used to be my gig up here in these hills. I cut down my share of trees. Now look at it. Wish we'd thought a little longer and harder about what we were doing in those days. Our logging crews were like nuclear-powered lawn mowers. Cut 'em down and drag 'em out. That's all we thought."

The other side of the road is a forest that hasn't been logged.

We get out and start walking. Raedawn kicks a clump of mud. "Looks like someone's been up here," she says.

61

"This mud must have fallen off a car not too long ago."

Uncle Dave says, "Hunters come up here all the time. And over the hills there are lakes stocked with fish."

I can see no point to the whole thing. On and on—forest on one side, Christmas trees on the other. We climb the hill for about ten minutes and I'm getting fed up. There's no end to the road.

Raedawn is charging ahead. She looks as if she expects to find something any minute, but I say, "I don't know about you guys, but from what I can see it doesn't look like anyone lives up here."

Uncle Dave says, "Not where it's been logged. But there might be a road heading off into the trees."

"Or we could walk for three days and never find anyone."

Raedawn says, "Stop being so negative, Vince. We've only been walking for a few minutes." She throws me an impatient look that irritates me.

Uncle Dave and I stop. "He's right," he says to Raedawn in my defense. "We could be on the wrong road. But I've been told that people have seen a pickup coming and going up here on a pretty regular basis."

I say, "Yeah, well, if we had a four-wheel or something, we could check it out." I'm hoping that Raedawn doesn't think we're going to check out the whole freaking mountain on foot.

"If we turn up nothing today," Uncle Dave says, "I'll borrow Sinclair's Toyota."

Raedawn says, "You won't have to. I know we're getting close to something."

We only walk a few more steps and she picks up a piece of paper. It's almost pulp from the rain.

"What do you think?" she says.

I say, "It looks like it might be a course outline." I can't read any words, but it looks familiar. There are columns and a heading across the top of the page.

Uncle Dave checks it out. "It could be. And I doubt hunters are going to drop school forms up here," he says.

She folds it up and says, "But Dune would. He probably brought it home the first day of school."

I have to admit the paper makes me think Dune might live somewhere up ahead, but who's to say how close. "So let's assume we've got the right place. How about we go back and get Sinclair's Toyota?" I say, hoping Sinclair's Toyota is in better shape than the old Dodge.

Uncle Dave says, "I think we ought to keep going. If they live up here, it's probably within walking distance of the bus stop. That means it won't be too much farther."

Raedawn agrees.

"Well then, how about you two go ahead and I just wait here until you come back?" I say.

Over the past two days I have had brief moments of interest in finding Dune. But this is not one of those moments. Two weekend mornings in a row I've been up by nine o'clock. That is more than anyone should expect from me.

Uncle Dave says, "Come on, young man. You can do it."

I'm thinking, Wait a minute, old man. Don't start with me. Not this early in the morning. Not here.

"I know I *can* do it," I say. Now I sound totally annoyed. "I'm just not sure I *want* to do it."

All of a sudden, like he's the boss of this adventure, he says, "We have no choice. We have to find him."

I say, "What difference does it make to you? You don't even know him."

"Vince, what's wrong with you?" Raedawn gets onto me like she's my mother.

I say, "Everything's wrong with me. We were coming up here for a drive, not a hike. We did that yesterday."

"Sorry, man. I definitely brought the wrong car, but I think we're on the right road," Uncle Dave says. "And we must be close."

"Why are you suddenly so interested in Dune anyway?" I ask. "Yesterday you couldn't have cared less. Now all of a sudden you're all over it."

We walk around a sharp turn in the road and he says, "Look at that, would you." Off to the left there's a road hacked into the forest. It's more of a trail than a road—like someone has taken an axe and slashed his way through the bush.

"Over here." Raedawn kneels down on the trail. "Some kind of vehicle has been here recently. You can tell from the tracks."

She's right. The grass has been chewed up since the last rain.

Uncle Dave says, "A small four-wheeler or an all-terrain by the look of it."

I want to quit because the two of them are really getting to me. But since we're making progress I decide to shut up. Raedawn and Uncle Dave walk ahead. He hasn't answered my question. He hasn't told me why Dune matters to him all of a sudden. But from behind he looks like a man on a mission.

The clouds are gone and the sun's streaming through the trees onto the trail. It's spongy—a thousand years of forest compost under my feet.

Raedawn says, "We're onto some-thing. This isn't a logging road. But someone's definitely using it."

"Looks to me like a private driveway," Uncle Dave says. "Only just big enough for a pickup."

They wait for me to catch up.

I don't really want to talk to them, but I say, "I'd rather be sleeping, but it does look like we're onto something now."

Raedawn grins and the two of them take off ahead.

I try asking the question again. "What makes you so interested in finding Dune, Uncle Dave?"

He doesn't slow down or even glance my way.

He says, "Raedawn."

"Yeah, I know. She convinced me too. But something hit you yesterday. At first you weren't interested at all and then you wouldn't let it go."

Raedawn looks confused.

She says, "What are you talking about?"

I'm a little shocked myself. It's not like me to wonder what's going on inside someone's head. That's totally Raedawn's department. But it's obvious that Uncle Dave isn't in this to find Dune. He's still got the hots for Dune's mom. That's what he's in this for. No question.

I ask, "Have you talked to Ocean lately?"

He says, "Like I was telling you yesterday. She dumped me like a hot potato. I don't think she's said hello to me in years."

Raedawn says, "That's sad. I see her once in a while and she looks like a nice woman."

"Oh, she's a nice-enough woman all right," he says. "But I wasn't a nice-enough man. Not to her or to my wife."

So he's got a reason to apologize. That's why he's hiking through this trail. What did he do all those years ago that made her drop him like a hot potato?

I'm just about to ask him, when the trail opens up onto a parking lot.

There's a long shed with a porch on one side and two all-terrain vehicles parked in front.

Raedawn bolts ahead.

Uncle Dave grabs both of us and pulls us into the bushes.

He says, "I don't feel good about this place."

"What the hell do you mean? We hike all the way up here to find Dune and now we're hiding?" I say.

He's not kidding around. I only have to look at his face to know we're in trouble.

He says, "We didn't find just someone. We've found a major operation."

Even Raedawn looks worried.

She says, "No way, Uncle. Do you really think so?"

It's not like we haven't heard about grow-ops in the hills. Weed flows fast and easy around town, but it's different looking directly at the place where tons of the stuff might be stashed at that very moment.

"That's not someone's house, Rae. That's a business."

We creep through the bush skirting the clearing. Up ahead there's a shack with a smokestack and plastic-covered windows.

Raedawn says, "Maybe that's where he lives. Let's go see."

"Slow down, girl," Uncle Dave says. "Not so fast."

It's amazing. The three of us sneak through the bushes past the cabin without making a sound. The adrenaline rush that comes with being afraid makes you do stuff you never could do otherwise.

We end up sitting on top of a bluff overlooking a small valley. Everywhere I look there are small groves of monster marijuana plants hanging with bud.

The whole place smells like you just opened a baggy.

"Holy crap. This is freaking weed paradise." I take a long whiff. "Incredible."

"Vince." Raedawn slugs my arm. "Don't talk like that."

Snap! Out of nowhere, it feels like the inside of my head blows out my ears.

A bullet shears the rock near Uncle Dave's feet and ricochets off a nearby tree. In a split second I'm down. I grab Raedawn on the way and pile on top of her. Uncle Dave crashes over the rock facedown into the bush.

He doesn't move.

"Dave." I spit the words through my teeth, trying to whisper loud enough for him to hear.

Another bullet cracks by. It shaves off a piece of the rock in the same place as the first.

Raedawn's shaking. "Vince. They've killed Uncle Dave."

From underneath me, she's looking down the hill to where he landed.

"I don't think so."

But I'm not sure. Maybe the ricochet got him. From what I can see, the first bullet hit the rock. The second one did too.

"Dave," I call again, hoping like hell that I'm right.

A third bullet cracks a rock on the other side of us.

I bury my face in Raedawn's jacket. She's crying, and for a few seconds I think I'm going to as well. If Uncle Dave is dead, we're next. I'm starting to panic.

I close my eyes as tightly as I can. I don't want to look, but I have to. I open one eye at a time. Uncle Dave's looking back at me with his finger to his lips. God, what a relief!

"Uncle Dave's okay," I whisper to Raedawn like I'm cool with everything. "But don't move."

Another two shots hit trees farther away. Then it's quiet.

Raedawn whimpers, "Vince, I'm so scared."

"Don't worry," I say. "We're gonna be okay."

I'm terrified. But Raedawn needs me, and I like that feeling.

After a few minutes, Uncle Dave hunches on his hands and knees and crawls like a crab up the rocks to where we are lying. I lift myself up and Raedawn slithers out from underneath me.

He says, "Are you guys ready? We gotta make a run for it."

"Uncle," Raedawn cries, "they'll kill us!"

"If they wanted to kill us, they would have already."

I say, "They want to scare us away. And I'm scared, so let's make them happy."

Uncle Dave agrees. "They could have killed us all by now, but they didn't.

It's almost time to harvest and they are protecting their crop. We gotta get out of here."

"What about Dune?" Raedawn sits up, keeping her head low. "We need to find him before we go."

She's amazing, that girl. As soon as she thinks we're not going to die, she's ready to start looking for Dune where we left off.

I'd have thought Uncle Dave would go along with her. Not now. He says, "Raedawn, you listen to me, girl. We're going to make a run for the trail, and we're not going to stop running until we reach the car."

She says, "But he's in trouble, Uncle. I know he is."

"We'll get the police out here," Uncle Dave says. "They can take care of him."

Chapter Eight

"On the count of three, Vince, Raedawn, you run ahead. I've got a bad hip, but I'll be right behind you."

I yank Raedawn's arm. We stand up together and take off. At first I'm dragging her behind me, but after a few steps she bolts ahead. My heart is pounding so hard it feels like it could bust through my ribs at any second. I expect to hear gunshots.

My life, like a speeded-up movie, shoots through my mind. Stupid stuff like Mom and Dad fighting, a grilled cheese sandwich I burned and a Speedo bathing suit I got for my thirteenth birthday.

Raedawn slows down and glances at me as we reach the cabin. I can't believe it. She actually wants to stop and look for Dune.

I say, "Don't even think about it," before she has a chance to speak.

Uncle Dave is nowhere in sight, but I can hear him smashing through the bushes.

We run by the shed, through the clearing and past the all-terrain vehicles. Raedawn is burning up the trail ahead of me. Her short legs are really moving.

Suddenly a dog appears out of nowhere. He's snapping at our heels like he's herding sheep. At first I think he's going to take my leg off.

Raedawn slows up a bit.

"Look at that dog," she calls over her shoulder.

He's a strange-looking mutt with long wiry hair and spots like a Dalmatian. He looks familiar, but I can't think of where I would have seen him before.

"That's Dune's dog," Raedawn gasps. "I know it is."

"Hurry up. He's not going to hurt us."

"I know Dune's around here, Vince. He's really close."

She slows down and is jogging beside me.

"How do you know it's Dune's dog?" I ask.

"Vince, we have to go back."

"Forget the dog, Raedawn."

"It's not the dog. It's Dune."

"Dune or the dog. Forget it. I'm not going back."

I'm ahead of her now. The weather has changed. The sun is gone. Raindrops

whipped up by the wind sting my face.
I'm grabbing my sides and gasping for
breath. Running all day on the basketball court is nothing compared to
running for my life. I feel like I'm going
to have a heart attack.

"They're on the vehicles," Uncle
Dave hollers when he comes into view.

The ATVs' engines are revving like
race cars.

"A couple of guys were running
behind me," he says. His face is red and
he is puffing away. "They could have
caught up with me easily if they wanted.
Then they jumped on their machines
to show a little muscle. I don't think
they'll hurt us, but I don't want to give
them anything to shoot at. I don't like
messing with bullets."

Raedawn ignores what he's saying.
"That's Dune's dog," she says. "Vince,
don't you recognize him from the painting
at school?"

Of course. That's where I've seen that mutt. There's a huge oil painting of the dog's face hanging outside the principal's office.

"You're right," I gasp. I'm having trouble talking and running at the same time.

We slow up a little to keep in step with Uncle Dave. The ATVs sound like a pack of mad dogs tied to a leash. They're staying out of sight, but they're pumping their engines. I figure Uncle Dave's right. They have no intention of killing us, but that doesn't mean we have time to hang around. The way those guys played with their guns, we could still catch a stray bullet.

Uncle Dave says, "Dune or no Dune. These guys want us out of here."

We pile into the car. We're soaking wet. Uncle Dave turns the key. *Click.* No engine noise.

Raedawn says, "Mom's been having trouble with the starter."

He turns the key again. "Good time to tell me now."

"Come on," she says, rocking back and forth as if it will help. "It'll start eventually."

After a few clicks the engine kicks in. We back up until we reach a place in the road wide enough to turn. Uncle Dave swings the car around and takes off.

"They're still chasing us," Raedawn screams. "Hurry, Uncle."

He says, "No worries, girl." He's as cool as anything now, although he's still breathing hard from all the running. "They're not really chasing us, Rae. At least they don't want to catch us. They are just making sure we don't stick around."

Two gunshots snap in the air, nowhere near us but loud enough to sting my ears. Uncle Dave is driving as fast as he can on the rough road. When it's obvious that we are scared and running, the ATVs wheel around and howl back up the road.

I'm shaking like a damn leaf. Raedawn is as white as I've ever seen her and silent, which is also a first.

Uncle Dave's in major pain—like an old man who's been roughed up on a street corner. At the highway, he turns toward town instead of our village.

"We're going to the RCMP. It's their job to take care of this."

A few minutes up the highway, he pulls over and stops the car.

"I gotta tell you, I got nothing left here, kids. I'm a glob of jelly. This old man hasn't worked out that hard for years. A short break is needed here or I'm going to have a heart attack."

I know how he feels. Gunshots have a way of sucking up the energy.

Even Raedawn's lost it. She's curled up in a ball with her head on my lap, sobbing.

It's completely silent—as if someone has switched off the power. No one moves. It's an opening for me to speak, so I say, "We're all in pretty good shape really. I mean, we're alive. For a while there I thought those guys were going to kill us all."

It doesn't have the desired effect. Raedawn starts crying more loudly, and that's the end of our conversation.

Chapter Nine

My head is full of stuff to say, but I keep
my mouth shut. Coming that close to
death makes you think. I wonder what
good my life has been up until now. And
what if I did die, what would people say
at my funeral? That Vince was a great
basketball player? Which is crap. Steve
Nash is great. I can barely shoot a hoop
compared to him. They'd say I was such

a nice guy, which is a load of crap as well.

In every way, up until now, my life's been pretty lame. At least it was before I met Raedawn. I didn't do anything until I knew her. I didn't think about much either. In fact, looking for Dune might be the first worthwhile thing I've done in my life, and we haven't even found him yet.

Raedawn's taken her braids out, and her hair is hanging over my lap. I stroke her hair. It's so smooth.

Cheesy as it sounds, I'm thinking that my life is only getting started. I guess looking death in the face does that to you.

We pull up in the parking lot behind the police station. Uncle Dave opens the door, picks up his legs with his hands and puts his feet on the ground.

He says, "I need a hand over this way. These old legs might not forgive me anytime soon."

Raedawn dashes around and stands beside him. I stand on the other side. Together we half lug and half push him through the door. A uniformed RCMP officer is in the waiting room.

"You hurt?" he says. "You need an ambulance?"

"No, no," Uncle Dave says. "We're here to make a report. A young man needs help up in the hills."

The RCMP officer throws us a look I've seen a million times before. It's the same one Dad has when he sees First Nations people—especially if they are in trouble. It's that they're-drunk-and-disorderly look.

We sit on a row of metal chairs outside a wicket. There's a woman on the other side of the glass, hunched over and talking on the phone.

The officer says, "She'll take care of you," and then he disappears into a back room.

I don't mind sitting for a while. I'm tired, but I can see as plain as anything that the woman's not talking business. I get up and stand in front of the glass.

When she finally glances my way, she lifts her chin. She says, "I'll be right with you," and then into the phone she says, "I gotta go. There's some guy here. I'll phone you back in a few minutes."

She says, "Yeah, can I help you?" like I'm cutting into her personal life.

"We need to see an officer. Some idiots up in the hills have just been shooting at us, and we're lucky to be alive. Can we talk to someone and make a report or something?"

"Yeah, sure. Hold on, I'll get someone."

She strolls into an office behind the reception area and says, "There's a couple of Indians and a white kid out here who look like they've been in a fight. Anyone here got time to talk to them?"

She doesn't keep her voice down, which I would have done if I had described us the way she did.

A man's voice says something. I can't make out the words.

"Yeah, probably," she responds. "They look like it."

I can't believe what's happening. We look like what? We look like we're drunk and disorderly?

She comes back into the room, and I'm standing with my tongue stuck to the roof of my mouth. If I say anything, they'll have to drag me out of there in handcuffs.

I've heard prejudice talk all my life. Dad's full of it. All his friends are full of it. I never took much notice of it until I met Raedawn. But hearing it directed at me, even if it is because I'm with Uncle Dave and Raedawn, makes it personal. It's not *them* the police won't listen to—it's *me*.

I collapse in a chair next to Raedawn.

She says, "What's taking them so long?"

"That woman just told someone there are two Indians and a white kid out here who look like they've been in a fight. They think we're drunk."

Raedawn's quick, but I've never seen her move so fast. By this time the woman is already on the phone again—laughing.

"Excuse me," Raedawn says. Her voice is loud enough so the guys in the back room don't miss a word. "There are not two Indians and a white kid out here who look like they've been in a fight. There are three human beings who have been shot at by a bunch of criminals who are growing and selling marijuana up in the hills. We would like some attention before someone gets killed."

Uncle Dave lifts his head and opens his eyes.

He says, "You've got a good point there, Rae," and closes his eyes again.

"I'm sorry, ma'am," the receptionist says. "We're really busy right now."

Raedawn says, "We can see how busy you are. Do you think we are too drunk to notice that you are deliberately ignoring us?"

Instantly an officer appears and sits next to Uncle Dave. She holds out her hand. "I'm Constable Shennihan," she says.

Uncle Dave says, "Dave Angus. Pleased to meet you."

"If you all could follow me, we'll talk in there." She points to a door at the end of the waiting room.

We help Uncle Dave hobble into the room and sit around a long table. She's got questions. Who are we? Where are we from? Why were we up in the hills? What happened? Who is Dune? Why do we think he's in trouble?

We fill out forms, sign our names and stand up to shake her hand.

She says, "Thank you for coming in. I think that's all we need from you."

"What do you mean, that's all you need from us?" Raedawn asks. "We came in because we needed something from you."

The constable looks at Raedawn as if she can't quite figure her out. I know how she feels. Raedawn never stops surprising me. The girl isn't afraid to say anything.

Constable Shennihan says, "Um, Rae…Rae…" trying to remember Raedawn's name.

"Raedawn." Raedawn leans forward. Short as she is, she's eye-to-eye with the cop. "Raedawn Angus. My questions are, what are you going to do now, and how quickly are you going to send someone up to that plantation to find Dune? We need to know or we will have to go back up there and find him ourselves."

"Oh no, Raedawn, don't do that. We'll send a car up there and take a look around," she says.

Uncle Dave asks, "And when will you get back to us?"

"We'll call you whenever we know something."

The room is quiet for a few moments. Raedawn is not satisfied. She crosses her arms and sits back in her chair. The constable picks up her papers and pats them into a neat pile. She turns to the door.

"I think you have missed our point," Raedawn says. "We've just been shot at. One of our friends is still up there. We believe he is in danger. Either you guys are going to go up there right now to find him or we are."

Constable Shennihan sits down. "I would not advise you to go back up there. It's not safe."

"We know it's not safe," Raedawn says. "We are the ones who were shot at. But that means Dune is not safe, and from what I've just heard from you, it doesn't sound as if you guys are in any big hurry to do something about that."

The constable finally understands what Uncle Dave and I already know—Raedawn is not going to give up.

She says, "Okay. I hear you. Here's my card. Call me anytime. I think I'll go up there myself. I'll let you know immediately."

The constable smiles for the first time since we arrived. "Thanks for your help. It's people like you who make our community a better place for us all."

Raedawn slams the door of the car.

"Yeah, I bet she really believes that," she says. "It's people like me who make our community better. She doesn't even listen to people like me."

Uncle Dave says, "Oh yes she did. Not the first time. That's what happens when you look like a couple of Indians and a white kid who have been in a fight. Dismissed. Ignored. But stick with it, like you did, Raedawn, and they gotta hear you. You spoke and that woman listened. I listened too. So did Vince. And everyone else in that office."

"Oh yeah, and thanks a lot to you two for helping me out. You didn't say a word."

"I would have, honey. If you needed me. But you didn't."

"I did so."

"No, you didn't. You were awesome."

She sucks in a deep breath and sighs.

Looking my way, she says, "What about you? Why didn't you step in and help me? You could see she wasn't listening to me."

Suddenly the whole thing has changed around. Raedawn is mad at me. Supposedly now I'm the one who's done something wrong.

I want to explode, although I'm not sure exactly why I'm so bent out of shape. I should have defended her, but I was as insulted as she was. Anyway, it's Raedawn who got me in all the trouble in the first place. She's the one who wanted to find Dune. She almost got us all killed. Maybe I'm missing something, but how does all that make me wrong?

I keep my cool and say, "Why would she have listened to me any better than she did to you?"

"She would have listened to you if you had said something."

"I doubt it."

"Yeah." Raedawn rolls her eyes in disgust. "You're white. White people don't ever listen to us."

Way to go over the edge, Raedawn. What the hell can I say to that? Let me try and get this straight. If you're white and hang out with Natives, white people treat you like crap—the same way they treat First Nations. And if you're white and hang out with Natives, you are to blame for every dumb-ass thing white people do and say. I need help trying to straighten this out in my head.

Lucky for both of us, Raedawn doesn't say any more the rest of the way home. Uncle Dave hums along to a Creedence Clearwater song. I steam inside and watch the trees. It's windy and spitting. I'm cold and I haven't had any lunch.

Chapter Ten

"What the hell is going on?" Dad's watching TV when I get up. "Take a look at that. We're on the six o'clock news. The cops are out there by the bridge."

I glance at the screen. There's Constable Shennihan, two RCMP trucks and the ATVs. I can't hear what they're saying because Dad won't shut up, but a couple of male officers have a big guy cuffed.

Dad says, "They made a drug raid up in the hills this afternoon. Gonna have themselves a couple of motorcycle mafia behind bars."

I catch the part when the reporter says they caught two major drug figures and brought three people in for questioning.

Before they finish reporting, Raedawn calls—obviously she's over the silent treatment she gave me all the way home in the car.

"Did you see? It's them, Vince. They got them."

"Yeah. I know. I'm watching the news."

"I am going to phone Constable Shennihan."

Dad's yelling. "Wait a minute. Were you snooping around up there in the hills? That Dune character, I guess he's one of these dope dealers?"

Raedawn's trying to get my attention on the phone. "What did he say about Dune?"

I would really like both of them to be quiet so I can hear the rest of the news report.

I say, "Dad, just shut up, will you? I'm on the phone with Raedawn."

"The hell with Raedawn. Sit down and tell me what you've been up to before the cops come to take you away."

"What did he say?" Raedawn asks.

"Who cares? Phone me after you talk to the cops."

"Bye."

"You know these guys?" Dad asks.

"Just shut up!"

He gets up and follows me into the kitchen. "Those damn guys shot at the police. And one of them was a lady cop. Why the hell did they send a lady cop up there? The hills are covered in marijuana plants ready to harvest. That stuff is worth millions. Can you imagine? Right here under our noses. Gangsters. And they send a lady cop."

Even if I did want to talk to Dad, how can I figure out what he's saying? I head for the stairs.

"Get back in here and explain yourself."

"Why should I? You don't listen."

He says, "I'm listening," and he sits back down and lights up a cigarette. "See, I'm sitting right here listening. I want to know what you and that damn girlfriend of yours have to do with these dope dealers."

"Nothing."

"Oh yeah? How long is it going to be before the cops show up here? Tomorrow night I'll be watching my son on TV with a bunch of Indians."

"That's what you're afraid of? That your damn racist friends will find out your son has a First Nations girlfriend?"

"I brought you up right, Vincent. You listen to me."

I lose it completely. "You brought me up to hate anyone who doesn't look like me. That's just damn wrong. You know what, old man? Things have changed. The way you think doesn't work anymore. Not with me."

"I'm telling you to stick to your own. That's all. No one is going to accept anything else. Not even the damn Indians accept it, Vince. I know what I'm talking about."

I flop on the sofa. Suddenly I'm breathing easy. I'm relaxed—the tension is gone. It's like after winning a big game. Clearheaded and on top of everything.

I say, "Okay, so if you're right and no one will accept Raedawn and me, then everyone has to change—including you. Because that's just wrong. You're a racist."

"Don't you call me a damn racist!"

I laugh. "What do you call it then?"

"It's the way it is."

The phone rings. It's Raedawn. We talk for a minute.

Before Dad has a chance to say anything else, I say, "Uncle Dave and Raedawn are picking me up in a few minutes. We're going to town to pick up Dune and his mother. They're at a homeless shelter."

Dad bolts up out of his chair. "You are doing nothing of the sort." He's standing in the middle of the room looking like a lost kid in his undershorts. For the first time I think he gets it. He finally realizes that he has no control over me anymore.

"I'll be home late. Tell Mom not to wait up for me."

"But, but…"

"Listen to me, Dad. A friend needs my help and I'm going to be there for her. It's the way it is."

I pick up my coat from the chair by the door. "Don't lock the door."

He says, "This is still my house." His shoulders droop, his mouth is slightly open. A cigarette is glued to his bottom lip. He looks like a dog that's just taken a beating. For a split second I feel pity for him.

It's dark when we reach the address Raedawn had scribbled on a piece of paper. It's a basement suite in an old dilapidated farmhouse not far from our school. Uncle Dave goes inside. It takes a while for him to come back out. He's walking behind Ocean and Dune.

Dune climbs in the backseat next to Raedawn. His mom sits in the front, leaning hard against the door, as far away from Uncle Dave as possible.

It's quiet. Uncle Dave's driving slow. I imagine the five of us are in a spaceship cruising through time and space. I'm waiting for someone to speak and bring us in for a landing on a day and a place that I'll recognize.

Uncle Dave breaks the silence. He says, "Dune Solomon Hunter," and that's it. It sounds as if he's making an introduction—like I should say Vincent Archibald Hardy, but I don't.

The rest of us wait.

After a while he says, "King David. Remember, Ocean? You always called me King David."

I think it over, and it makes no sense to me. What's with the King David? Is it some game the two of them used to play together? It sounds sort of creepy to me.

I can't see Ocean's face, but if you can tell what someone's thinking from the back of their head, then I'd say she's totally uncomfortable. Her shoulders are hunched forward and turned away from Uncle Dave. Her hand keeps swishing her hair back as if she doesn't really want her face uncovered. I can't tell if she even heard what he said. I glance over and can't see Dune's face either. He's slid into his hoodie and has his eyes closed.

Raedawn is sitting up straight and leaning into the front seat. "What do you mean King David?" she asks.

Uncle Dave ignores her.

He says to Ocean, "Do you still read the Bible?"

"Yes, but not as much as I used to."

"Uncle, what does the Bible have to do with this?"

"Didn't I ever give you that book to read, Rae?"

"No, now tell me what you are talking about."

Uncle Dave takes his time and says, "King David is a famous king in the Bible. He had a son named Solomon."

Chapter Eleven

It turns out that Ocean ran away from a strict religious family when she was sixteen. She met a couple of hippies and they ended up camping on the beach near the reserve. It was love at first sight when she met Uncle Dave, and she thought they were going to live happily ever. The same day she learned she was pregnant, she also learned that Uncle

Dave was married. Heartbroken and embarrassed, she ran away again. She headed to the mainland until Dune was born. Once she saw him, she decided she wanted to raise him close to his people, which apparently didn't include his father. I think she messed the whole thing up right from the start. But I keep my mouth shut.

There are too many holes in the story for Raedawn.

She says, "Were you ever going to tell Dune or Uncle Dave?"

"Yes, when the right time came. And it never came. Until today and I knew who I needed to call."

"You mean you called Uncle Dave to come and pick you up?"

"Yes, I had to tell him my secret. Well, it isn't really my secret, is it? Dune is his son."

Raedawn says, "Were you too afraid of him to tell?"

"No, I was in love with him."

I confess that stories like this one, on TV or in a movie, usually bore the hell out of me. Girl meets guy. Girl falls in love. Guy screws up. It might be that I'm getting older or that I know Raedawn better, but now I'm getting the same feeling I get when I think about the dog I hit with Dad's pickup. I didn't kill it, but that dog is still lame to this day. I can't see that thing limping down the road without getting tears in my eyes.

I'm not as bad as Raedawn. She's got tears streaming down her face. She's wiping her nose with the back of her hand. Then, as if she hadn't thought of the most obvious part of the whole thing, she says, "Dune, that makes you my cousin."

He's crawled out from under his hoodie now that the story is out.

He says, "I guess you're right."

Ocean says, "I'm so sorry for being unfriendly in town. Whenever I saw you I had to turn away. I was afraid if I didn't, I would tell you everything."

Uncle Dave says, "Why didn't you? I mean, why didn't you tell me everything?"

"I wasn't ready. I made one mistake running away from you and another avoiding you. One bad decision after the other made it more difficult each time I saw you."

Ocean's sobbing. Uncle Dave's stroking her arm. Raedawn's sputtering. Dune's got his hand around her shoulder. The air's getting stuffy in the car. If I could climb out the window I would. I can't face another forty minutes with all the sentimental junk oozing all over the place.

"I didn't intend it to turn out this way," Ocean says.

I say, "Was one of those guys they arrested today your boyfriend?" Once the words come out I want to reach out and stuff them back in my mouth. Everyone is feeling all warm and fuzzy with each other, and I open my mouth and screw it up.

"Oh my god, no!" she gasps. "No. No. No. Of course that's what you would think. Oh no."

She tells us the rest of the story. When they were evicted from the shack down by the beach (it turns out it was the one Raedawn and I found), she and a few others moved up the hill. Two of her friends started growing marijuana.

She says, "I didn't agree with them, but I had nowhere else to go. Dune and I had a house, and I loved living in the hills. They lived their life and I lived mine. As long as I could do my art and raise my son, that's all I wanted.

"That wasn't such a good decision either. My friends started hanging out with some bad guys. They made some nasty business deals and owed a bunch of money. The guys who got arrested today came from Montreal to force my friends to pay up. Of course all they had was their crop, which was worth ten times more than what they owed those creepy guys. Anyway, they had an ugly fight a few weeks ago. Needless to say, my friends got the worst of it. The biker guys tied them up, and they've all been living in the shed. They were going to do the same to us, but we promised we wouldn't go out of the house. They kept shooting off that damn gun. They said they wouldn't kill us unless they had to—unless we went outside. They didn't care if we saw them. They had tickets to Paraguay. They said that as soon as the bud was harvested they were out of here and no one was going to find them."

Dune says, "That's when you guys changed their plans."

Chapter Twelve

We sit at the table—same places as usual. Dad at one end, Mom at the other and me on the side facing the window. Mom loads my plate with spaghetti.

They eat and say nothing. I decide I better do what Raedawn wants me to or I'll never hear the end of it.

I say, "Raedawn asked me to invite you to an event that's happening on the reserve."

"Oh," Mom says.

Dad keeps eating.

"Uncle Dave is welcoming Dune home."

He looks up and says, "Who the hell is Uncle Dave? You don't have no Uncle Dave."

Mom clears her throat, which is what she does when she's got the feeling Dad is going to say something she will regret.

"Raedawn calls him Uncle Dave, so I do as well."

"Are you married? Is her family your family now?"

I wonder why no one has told him not to talk with his mouth full.

"You got new family now, do you?" Chewed noodles and hamburger spray down his chest and onto his plate.

I say, "Don't talk with your mouth full."

He wipes his mouth with his sleeve and stuffs another forkful in his mouth.

I look out the window. "Dave Angus," I say. "He's putting on a celebration to welcome Dune home."

"Finally claiming the kid, is he? And gets his old chick in the same deal. She's not what she used to be, but she's as good as he's going to get."

I want to strangle him.

Mom says, "The talk around town is that woman was pretty wild when she was young. And then who knows what those people were doing in the bush. I don't even want to think about it."

She tightens her lips. I can tell that's exactly what's she doing—thinking about it.

"She doesn't sound wild to me."

"Oh, Vincent, you don't know the half of it," Mom says, putting her fork neatly on the side of her plate and tapping her lips with her napkin.

I say, "I know more about her than either of you."

Dad scrapes his fork along his plate and says, "You think you know everything, young man."

I can tell this conversation is going the same place a million other conversations have gone before—nowhere. I push back from the table. I'll finish supper in my room.

I say, "The two of you can think and say whatever you want. The fact that you are wrong doesn't seem to matter to you, and you know what? I don't give a crap about what you think."

"Oh yeah?" Dad's cracking open a beer. "Well, I'll tell you something you might want to remember. What happens in this house is up to me, and I'll say and do whatever the hell I want to."

I say, "And so will I."

"And so you won't."

"Or what? What'll you do, old man? Kick me out?"

"Don't tempt me, boy."

Mom does a double throat clear. She's thinking about the day my older brother, Ronny, stormed out the front door—I know it. Dad said the same thing to him, and we haven't seen him since.

"You and mom are invited to a celebration, Saturday at four o'clock, at the community center. Uncle Dave is welcoming Dune home. He is announcing to the community that Dune is his son. Uncle Dave moved into Raedawn's place and gave his place to Ocean and Dune. Raedawn wants you guys to come. Don't ask me why."

I leave my plate on the table and go downstairs.

Chapter Thirteen

Raedawn and I, her mom and a few other people decorate the hall with cedar boughs and *Welcome Home* banners. We cover one wall with Dune's artwork that Raedawn borrowed from the school. She puts the carved pole we found near the beach on a table next to the art. Above the display she hangs another banner that says *Meet Our Community's*

New Artist. By the time we're finished,
the place looks like an art gallery.

It's warm in the room. Streaks of sun
light up the place. I haven't done much
decorating in my life. I guess, when I
think about it, I haven't even been to a
community celebration. I like the way it
feels to be part of something.

By 3:45, people begin to show up.
I recognize a few teachers and Ruby,
from the store, and her boyfriend. There
are lots of people from the reserve and a
couple of geeky-looking white kids.

Dune and Ocean get there about four
o'clock and sit near the art display at
the front of the room. Raedawn's mom
directs Raedawn and me to sit next to
Dune. Uncle Dave is beside Ocean,
and Raedawn's mom is at the end of
the row next to him. We're facing the
crowd as if we're at the head table at a
wedding. I can't remember ever being
more conspicuous.

I whisper, "How about I go sit at the back?"

Raedawn says, "No way, Vince. You are staying right where you are. Isn't this the greatest?"

"Yeah, I mean, no. I don't like sitting up here."

"Vince, this isn't about you. It's about Dune."

Which is my point exactly. Let him sit in front of everyone. But I decide not to say any more.

Ocean's hair is tied back. She's wearing jeans and boots and doesn't look like as much of a hippie as she usually does. Old as she is, it's not hard to tell that she was hot when she was young. Uncle Dave has his arm across the back of her chair.

The room is packed when three men and a woman come in holding drums. They line up facing us and start beating really slowly. After a few

Sylvia Olsen

minutes they sing—no words. It's more
like a chant than a song. They speed it
up and a young kid with streaks of red
paint on his face charges into the room
from the back door. He's got on a pair of
shorts and a black velvet jacket covered
with wooden paddles hanging in lines.
He swooshes around the room like a bird.
The paddles clack in a sort of musical
rhythm. He dances until the drummers
stop and then they all leave the room.

I look around thinking that maybe
the thing's over. People are starting to
shuffle around. No one appears to be in
charge of the crowd.

Finally Uncle Dave gets up and turns
on a stereo. The guy's playing acoustic
guitar and singing folksy stuff about
the ocean and mountains and clear-
cuts. When the song is over, everyone
sits and waits. If I'd been running this
thing, I'd have gotten an MC—someone
to take charge.

That's when I get the shock of my life. Mom walks in the door with Debbie, our neighbor, and her daughters, Sherry and Millie. The girls walk right in and sit with some of the guys from the reserve. It's obvious Mom and Debbie aren't sure what to do, so they huddle together against the back wall.

Uncle Dave stands up.

He says, "That was Dune singing. He was playing the guitar as well. And he wrote the song."

Uncle Dave's obviously enjoying himself.

He points to the wall and says, "This is Dune's artwork."

He sits back down and flips on the stereo again. "This is another one of Dune's songs."

I can't believe my ears. It's a ballad about a dog, a mutt with spots that doesn't look like the other dogs.

It sounds professional—as good as you'd hear on the radio.

At the end, Uncle Dave stands up again. He takes Dune by the hand and pulls him up beside him.

He says, "This is Dune. My son."

He takes Ocean's hand and pulls her up.

"This is Ocean. Dune's mother. I want you all to welcome them into our community."

The crowd begins to clap. He raises his hands to quiet them down.

"I didn't know I had a son. I still don't know very much about him. But as you can see and hear, he is an incredible human being. I'm going to get to know him now. And I want you to get to know him as well. We started this ceremony with a traditional Coast Salish welcome song. Because that's where Dune comes from and that's an important part of who he is.

Today we're going to hear some other things about him as well."

One by one, people stand up and talk about Dune.

Mrs. Moran, the art teacher, says that on the first day of class in grade nine, Dune brought a portfolio of sketches that will one day be in an art gallery or museum. He's that good, she says.

An old woman from town remembers that Dune had meningitis when he was in grade three. He and his mother stayed with her so he could be close to the hospital. It was the first time he had seen a TV and he was amazed. He told her he believed in magic.

A long-haired guy who taught Dune how to play the guitar says Dune was better than him by the time he was twelve.

A woman who looks like Ocean says she helped Dune into the world and that he came out smiling.

An elder from the reserve tells the story of Dave's family. He explains the Coast Salish names of Uncle Dave's grandparents and great-grandparents. He describes how Dune is related to almost every family on the reserve and to other First Nations people in town and up the coast.

Uncle Dave's mother is crying when she talks. She says she has many grandchildren, but she always wanted Dave to have children. Everyone laughs when she describes Dave as a teenager. He was wild, and in those days she was afraid he would give her many grandchildren. She hugs Ocean and welcomes her into the family. Anyone, she says, who mothers her grandchildren is a daughter of hers.

Raedawn jumps up and throws her arms around Dune. "I have another cousin," she says. "I am so proud of you, Dune. Finding you wasn't easy, but it was worth it."

When she sits down, everyone looks at Dune.

They all start shouting, "Speech. Speech."

His chin is hanging on his chest. I sure don't envy him right now. If I were him, I'd be running for the door.

He takes a while and then stands up.

He says, "Thank you all. I'm kind of overwhelmed. And I'm not much of a speaker. But I wrote a song last night. And if you want, I'll sing it for you."

He sits down.

I am a traveler
I go from blood to blood
I wander through the woods inside
I sail on oceans men have cried
I run from cities where children died
They ask me, Where are you from?
They wonder from whose people I
    have come
I tell them I am from the ground

I am a human who has found
The red earth spongy to my feet
The cedars that the heavens meet
The wind that plays to us its call
The rain that gives life to us all
I am from you and you from me
I am as mixed up as can be
But I will sing to you my song
And I don't think blood can be wrong

He puts his head down and then looks up and laughs. He says, "That's all I have. I'm not sure how the rest of the song goes."

Sylvia Olsen is the author of *Yellow Line*, an Orca Soundings novel that introduced the characters from *Middle Row*. *Yellow Line* was an International Youth Library White Raven Award winner. Sylvia has lived on Tsartlip Reserve near Victoria, British Columbia, for almost thirty-five years.

orca soundings

For more information on all the books
in the Orca Soundings series, please visit
www.orcabook.com.